The Clever Tortoise

Gerald Rose

CAMBRIDGE
UNIVERSITY PRESS

One day, the elephant said to the tortoise,
"I'm going to step on you."

The tortoise said, "No, you're not.
I'm as strong as you are."
The elephant laughed.

"I'll show you how strong I am,"
said the tortoise. "You hold the end of
this rope.

4

I'll hold the other end of the rope. When
I say 'Pull', we'll both pull. I'll show you
that I'm as strong as you are."

The tortoise ran behind the trees,
and picked up the other end of the rope.

The tortoise said to the hippo, "I'm
as strong as you are."
The hippo laughed.

"I'll show you how strong I am," said
the tortoise. "You hold the end of this rope.

I'll hold the other end of the rope. When
I say 'Pull', we'll both pull. I'll show you
that I'm as strong as you are."

The tortoise ran into the trees. Then
she shouted, "PULL!"

The elephant pulled and the hippo pulled.

The hippo pulled and huffed and puffed.

The elephant pulled and huffed and puffed.

Snap! The rope broke. The hippo
fell into the river.

And the elephant sat down with a thump.

"See, I *am* as strong as you are,"
laughed the tortoise.